9780887080418

LINCOLN SCHOOL
OAK PARK, IL

Copyright © 1987 Yoshi.
Book design by Michael Neugebauer

This edition is reprinted by arrangement with Simon & Schuster
Books For Young Readers, Simon & Schuster Children's Publishing Division.

**Copyright © 1987 by Yoshi.
All rights reserved.**

Printed in U.S.A.

Printed by SRA/McGraw-Hill.

LIBRARY OF CONGRESS CATALOGING IN PUBLICATION DATA

Yoshi.
Who's hiding here?

Summary: A rhyming text explores animal camouflage, while die-cut pages reveal the animals hiding throughout the book.
1. Toy and movable books–Specimens. [1. Camouflage (Biology)–Fiction.
2. Animals–Fiction. 3. Stories in rhyme. 4 Toy and movable books] I. Title.
PZ8.3.M69Wh   1987   [E]   86-25455

Yoshi

Who's Hiding Here?

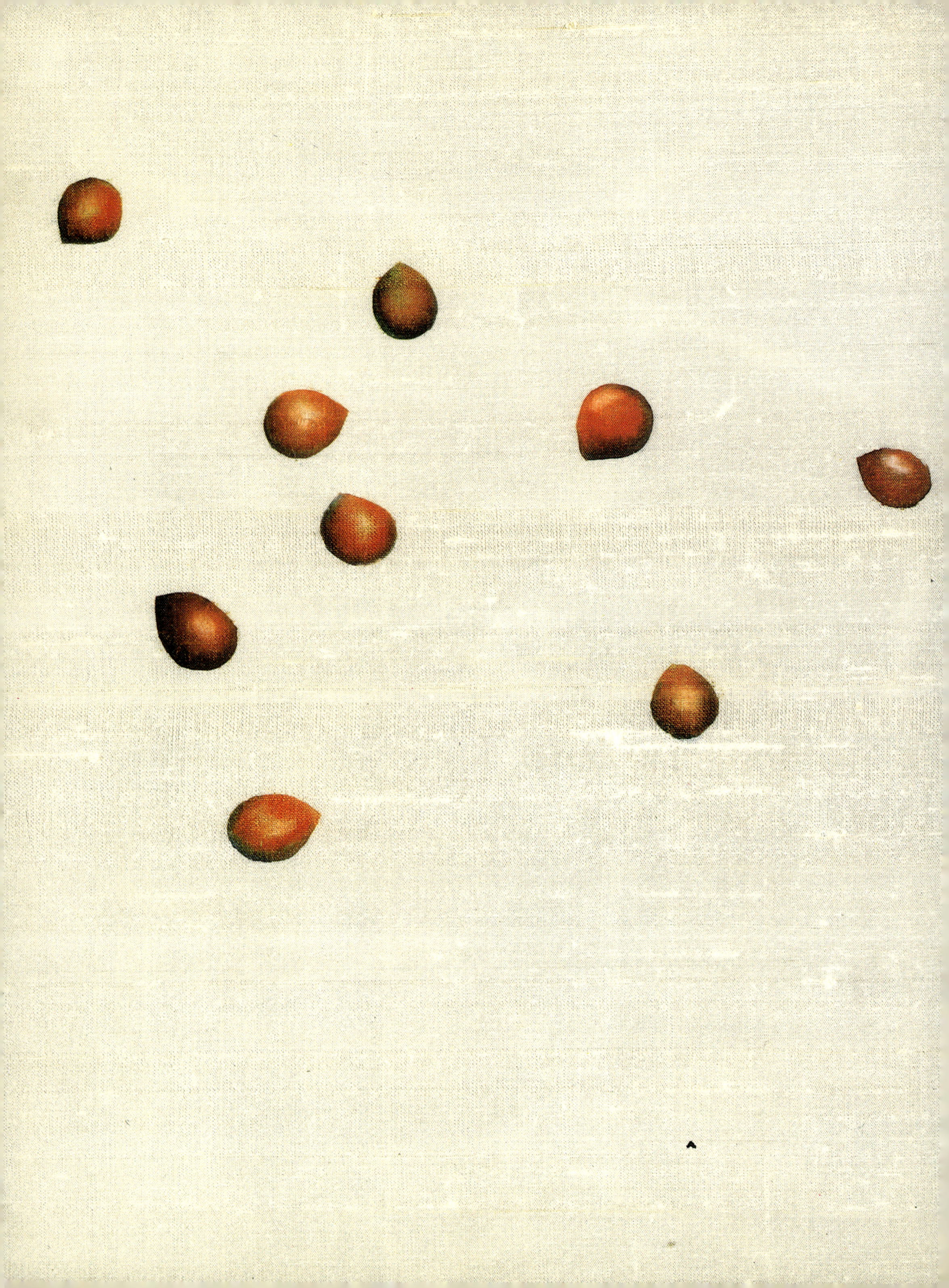

Snow has fallen,
crisp and bright.
But I see red
as well as white.

Who's hiding here?

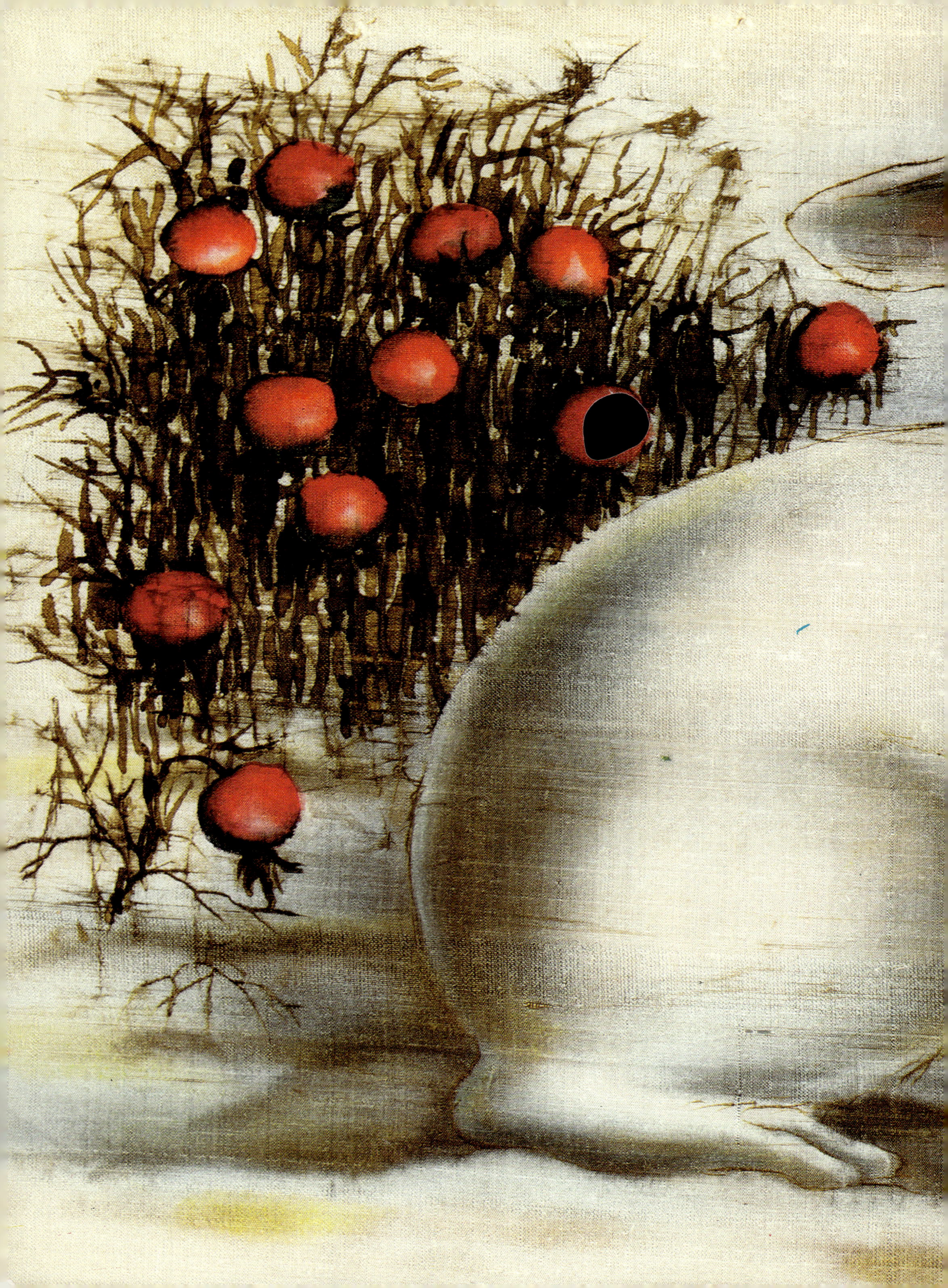

A white rabbit

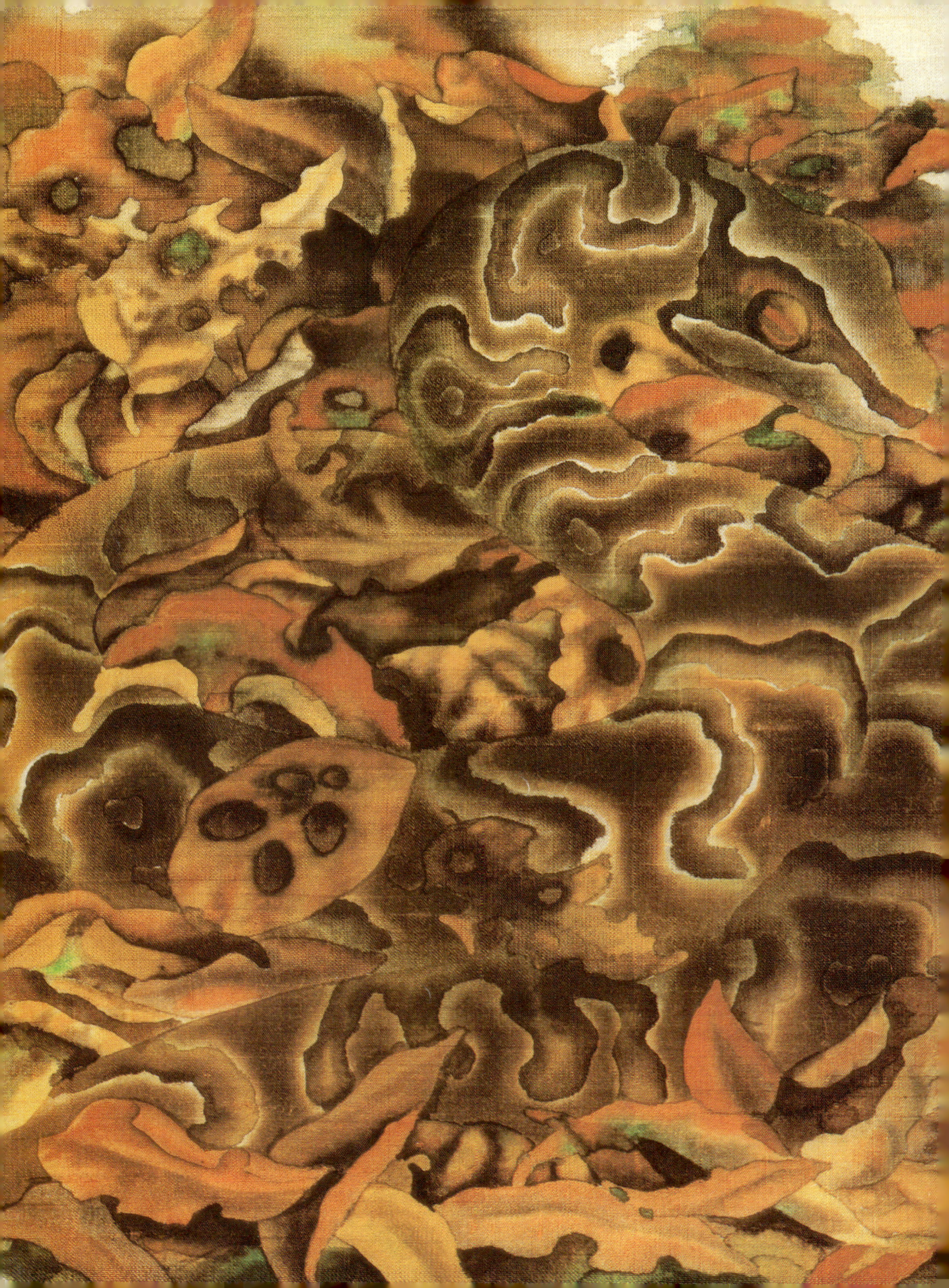

Among the leaves
of gold and green
someone hopes
he can't be seen.

Who's hiding here?

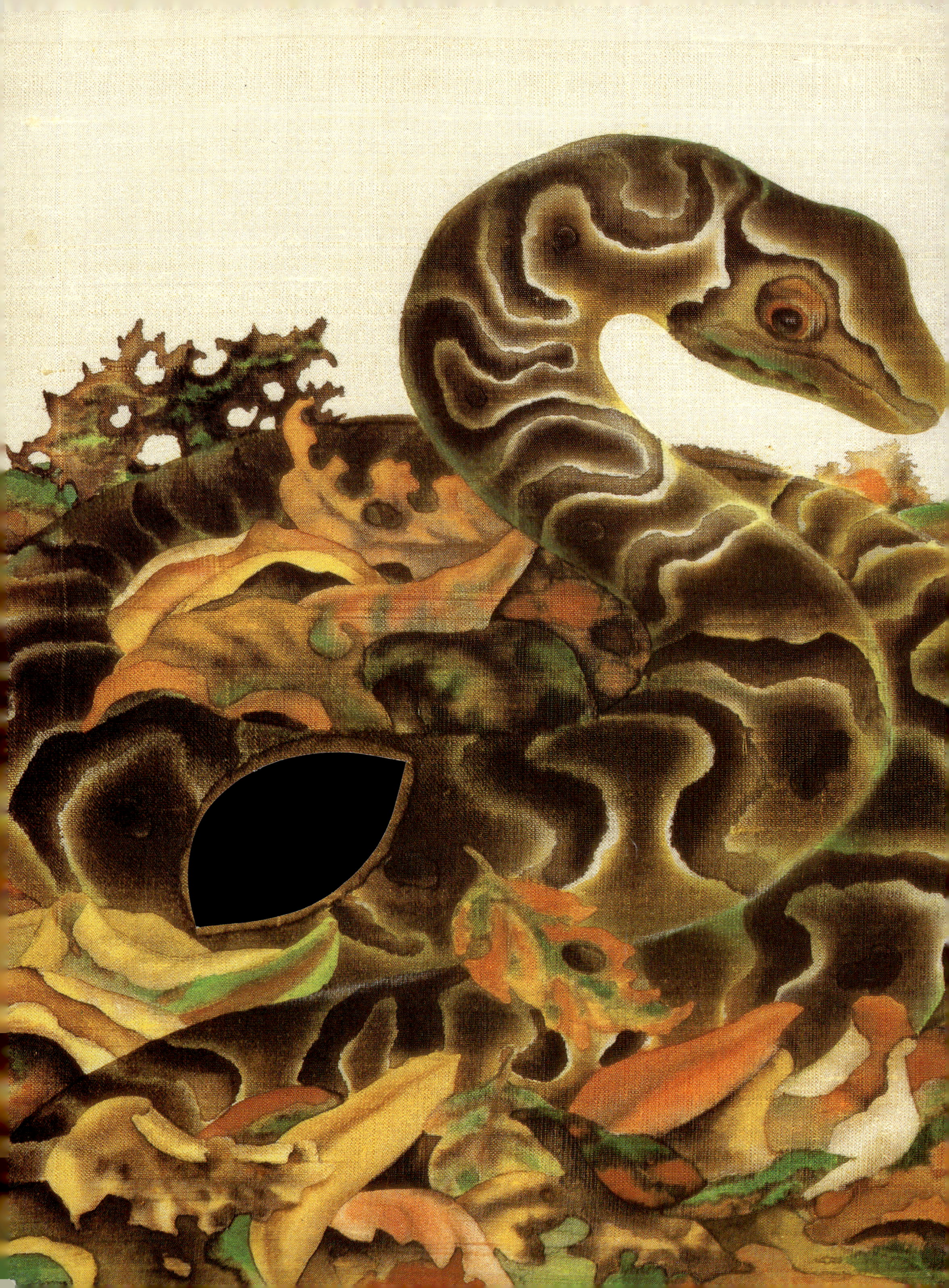

A frog and a snake

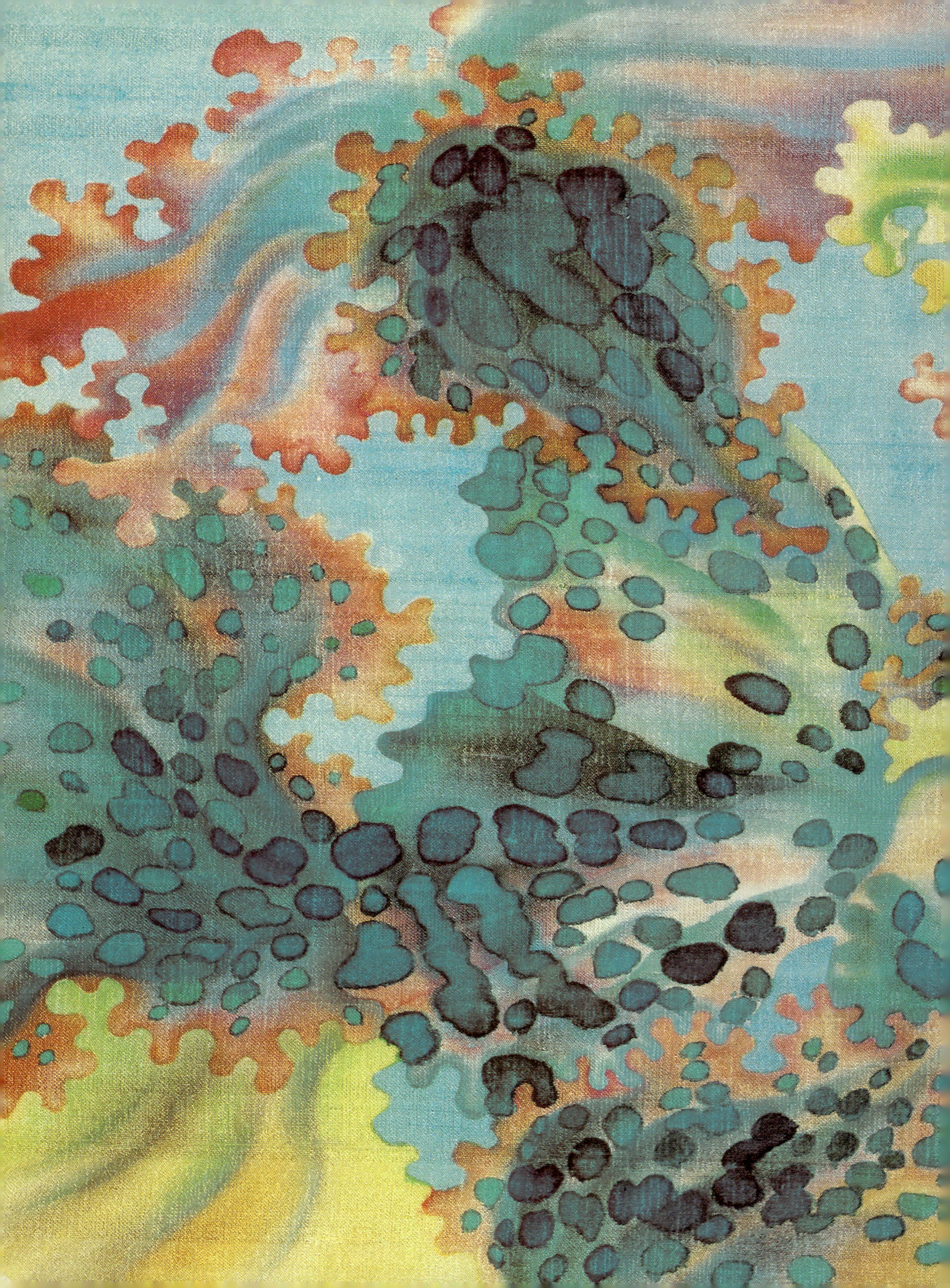

Rainbow splashes,
lots of dots.
Some are flowers,
some are not.

Who's hiding here?

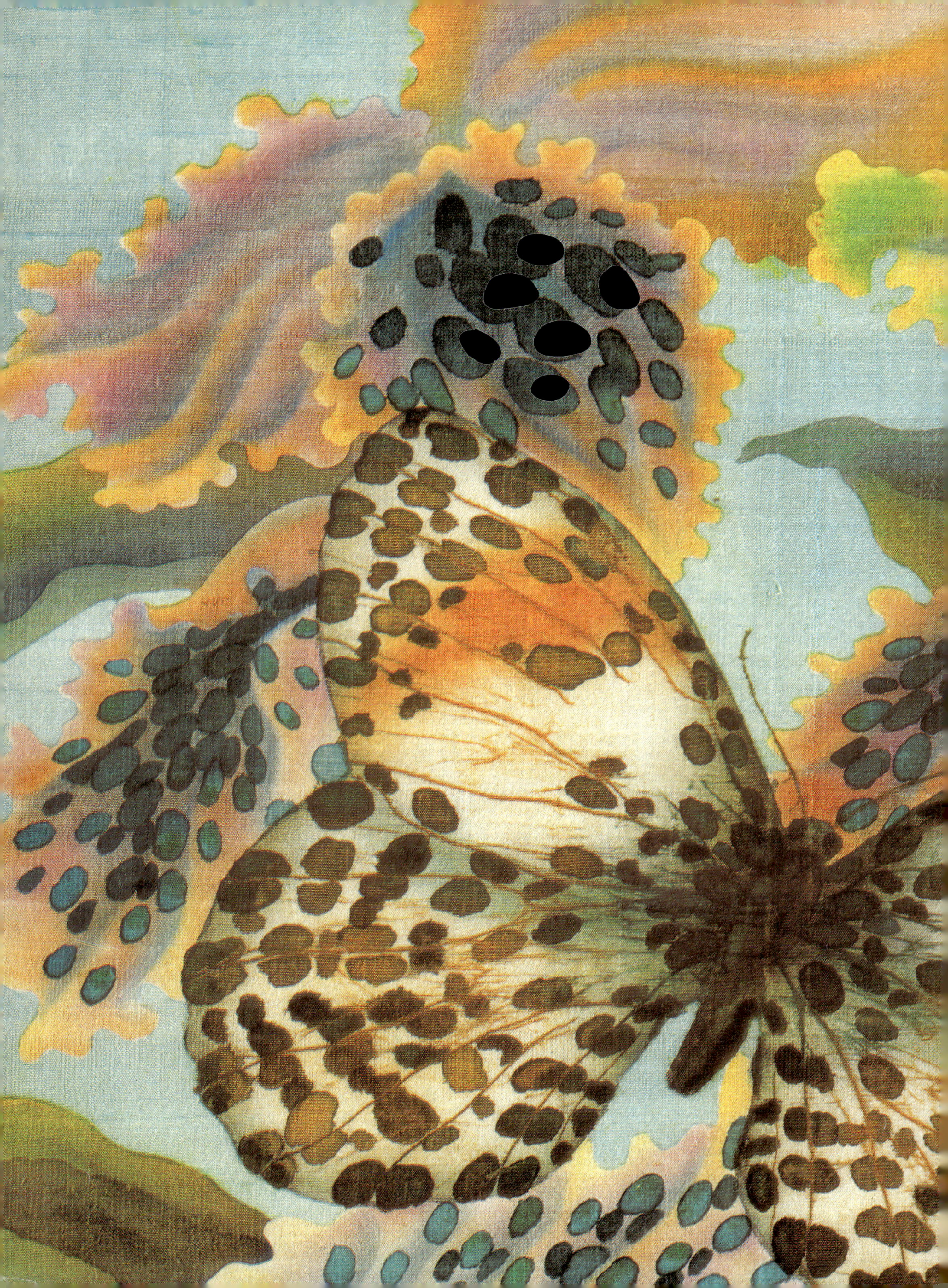

A butterfly and a beetle

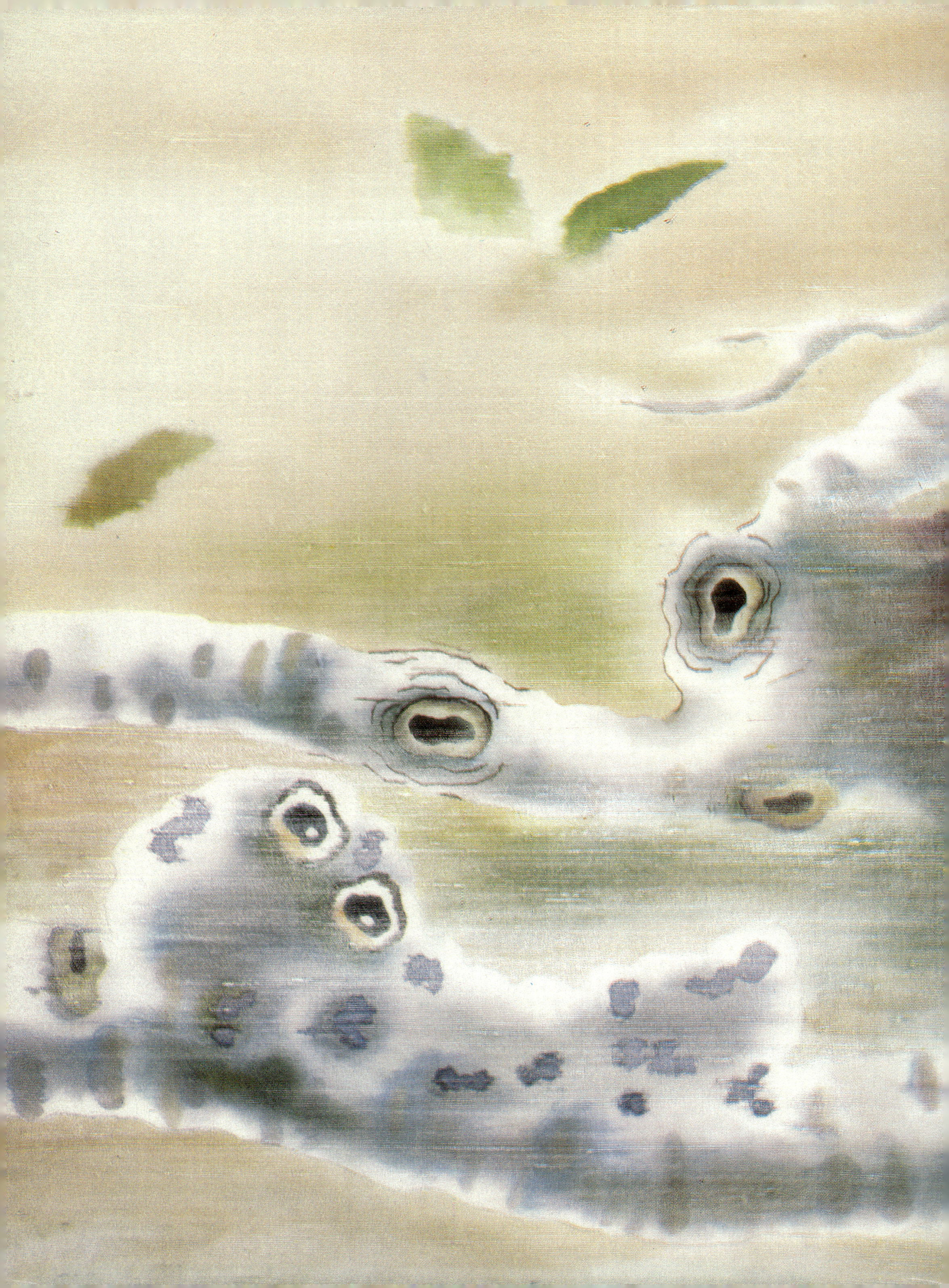

Eyes are blinking
on the log.
Eyes are winking
through the fog.

Who's hiding here?

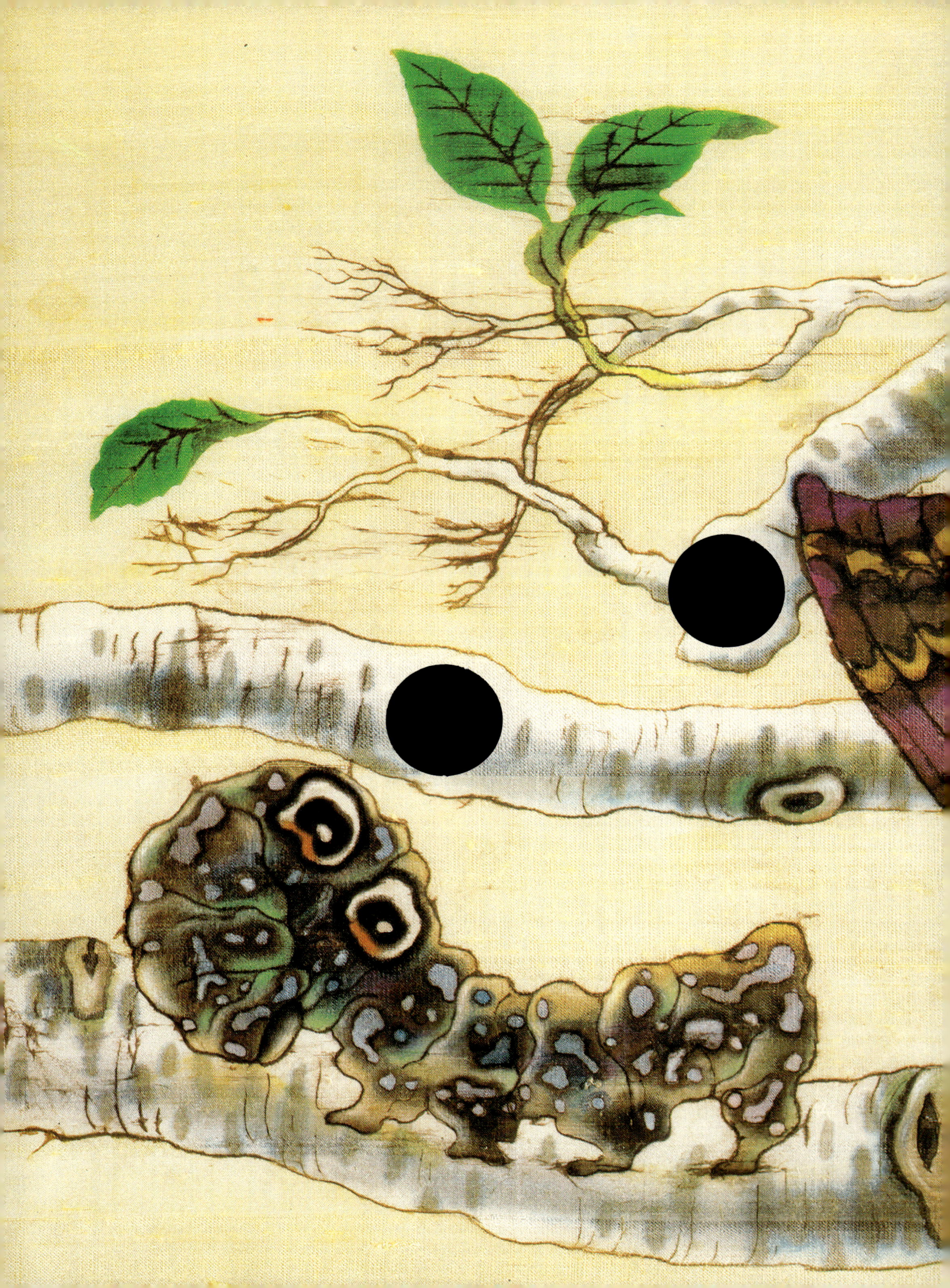

A moth and a caterpillar

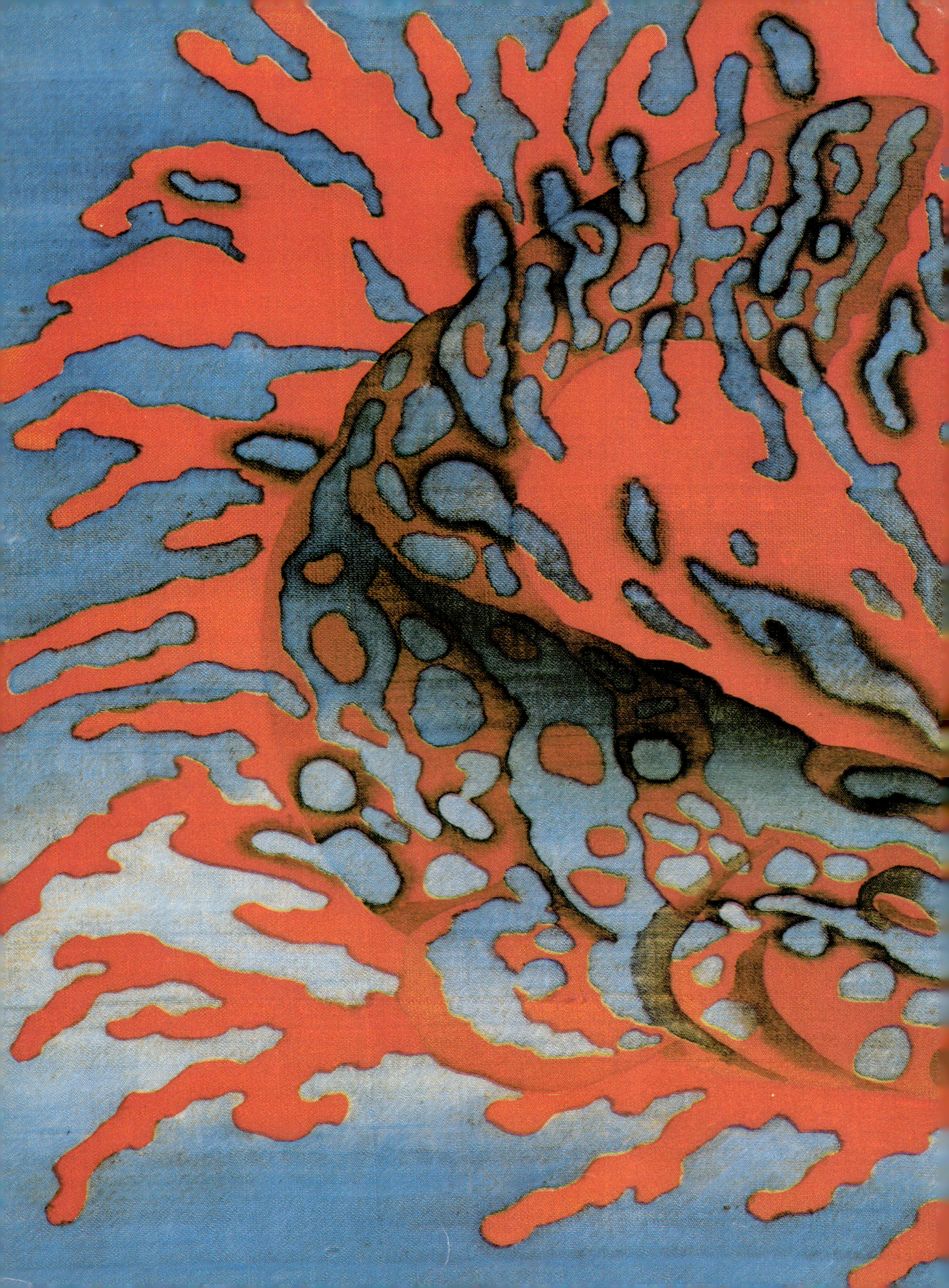

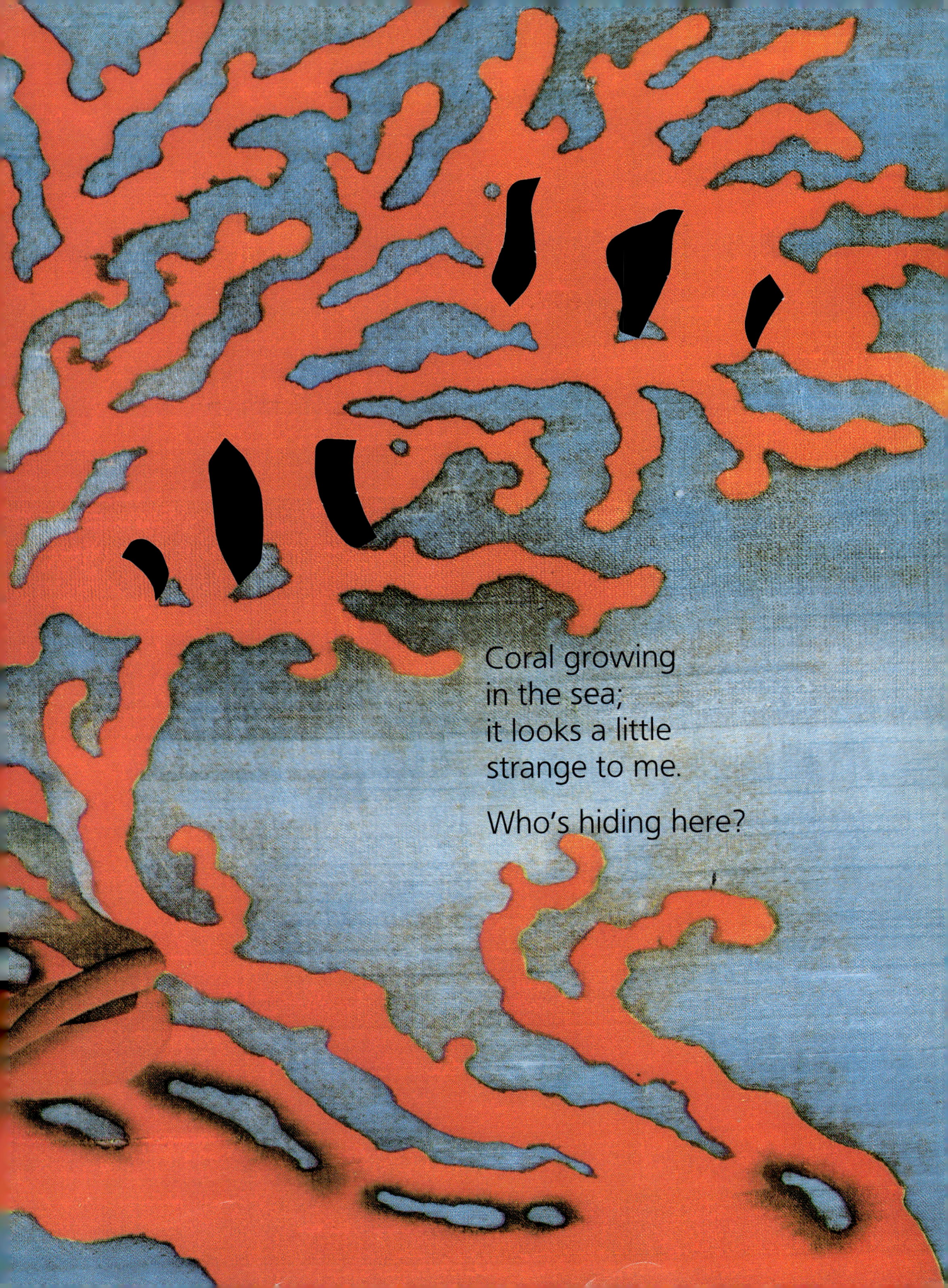

Coral growing
in the sea;
it looks a little
strange to me.

Who's hiding here?

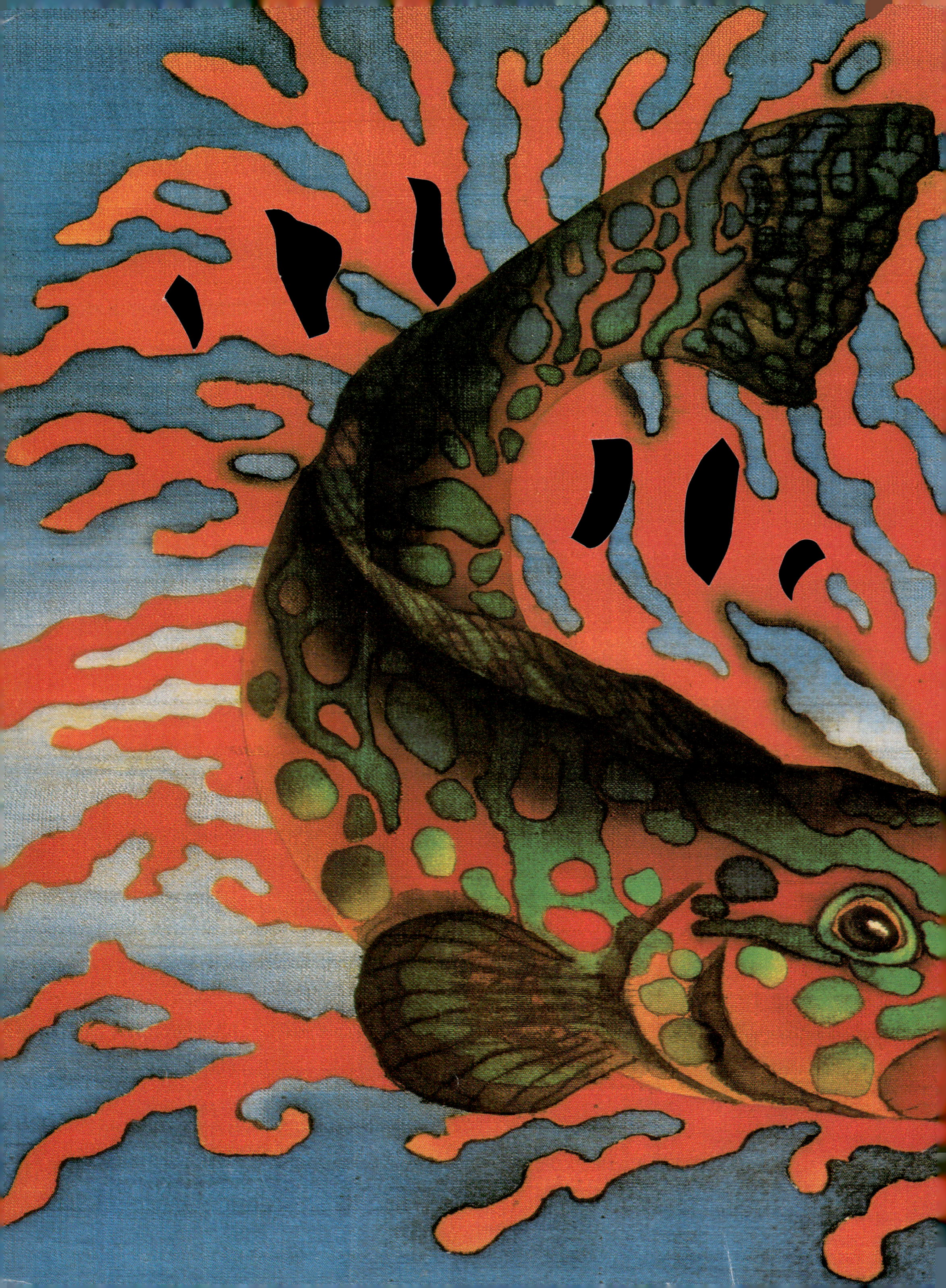

One big fish and two little fish

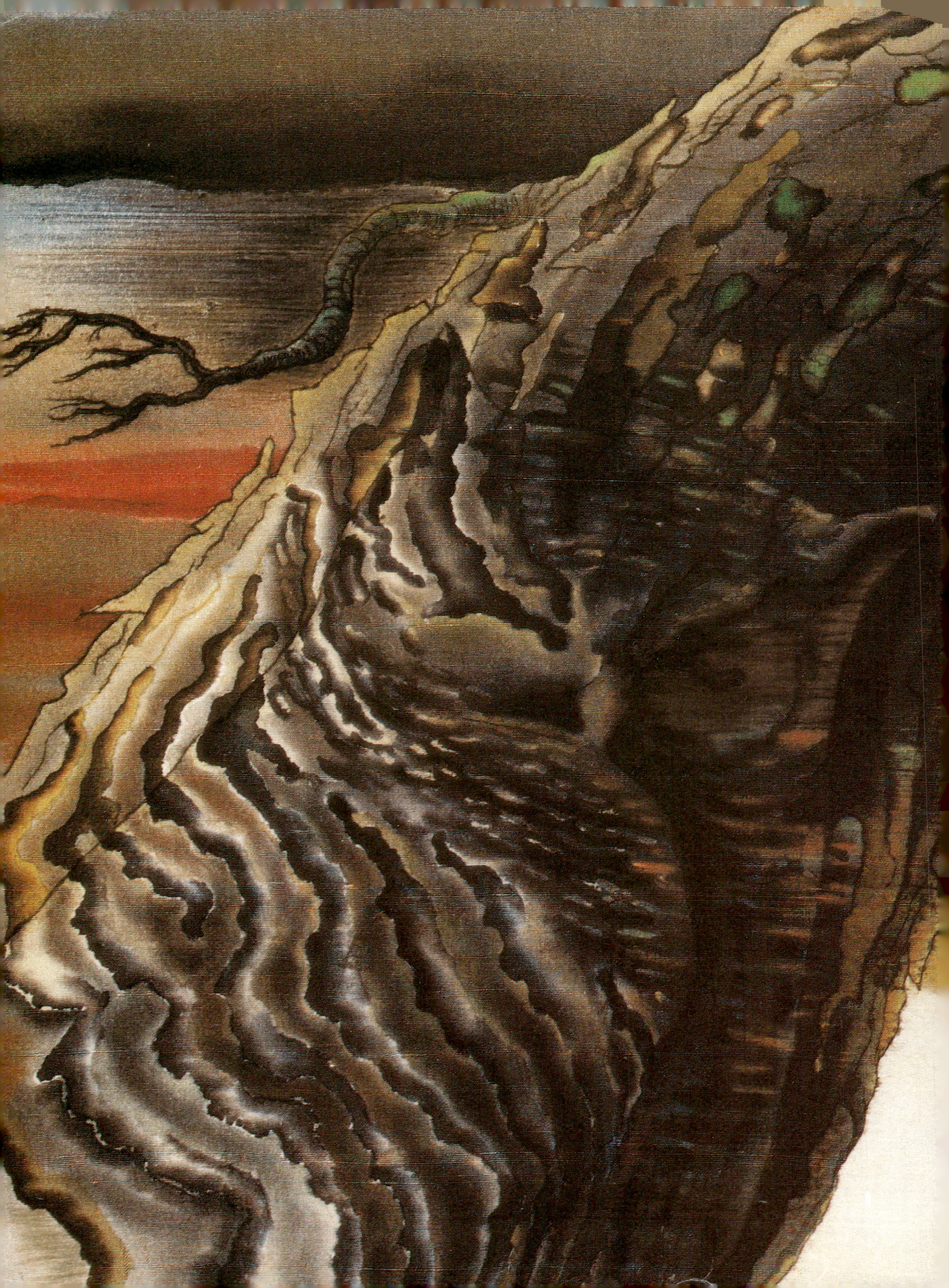

A stormy sky,
an old bent tree;
it's very dark —
I can't quite see.

Who's hiding here?

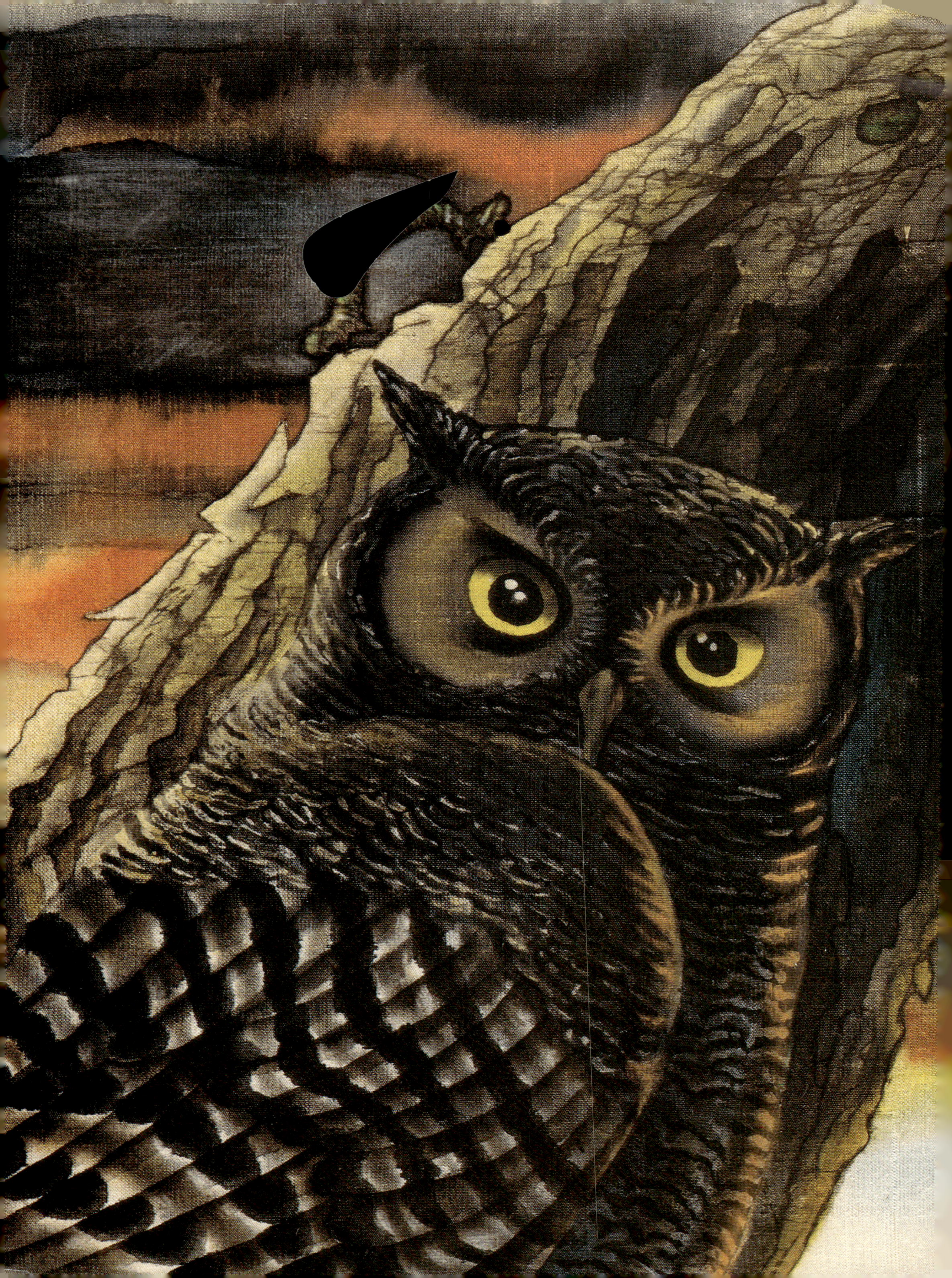

An owl, a moth, and a caterpillar

Golden stars are
sharp and bright.
But look – <u>two</u> moons!
That can't be right!

Who's hiding here?

A black cat

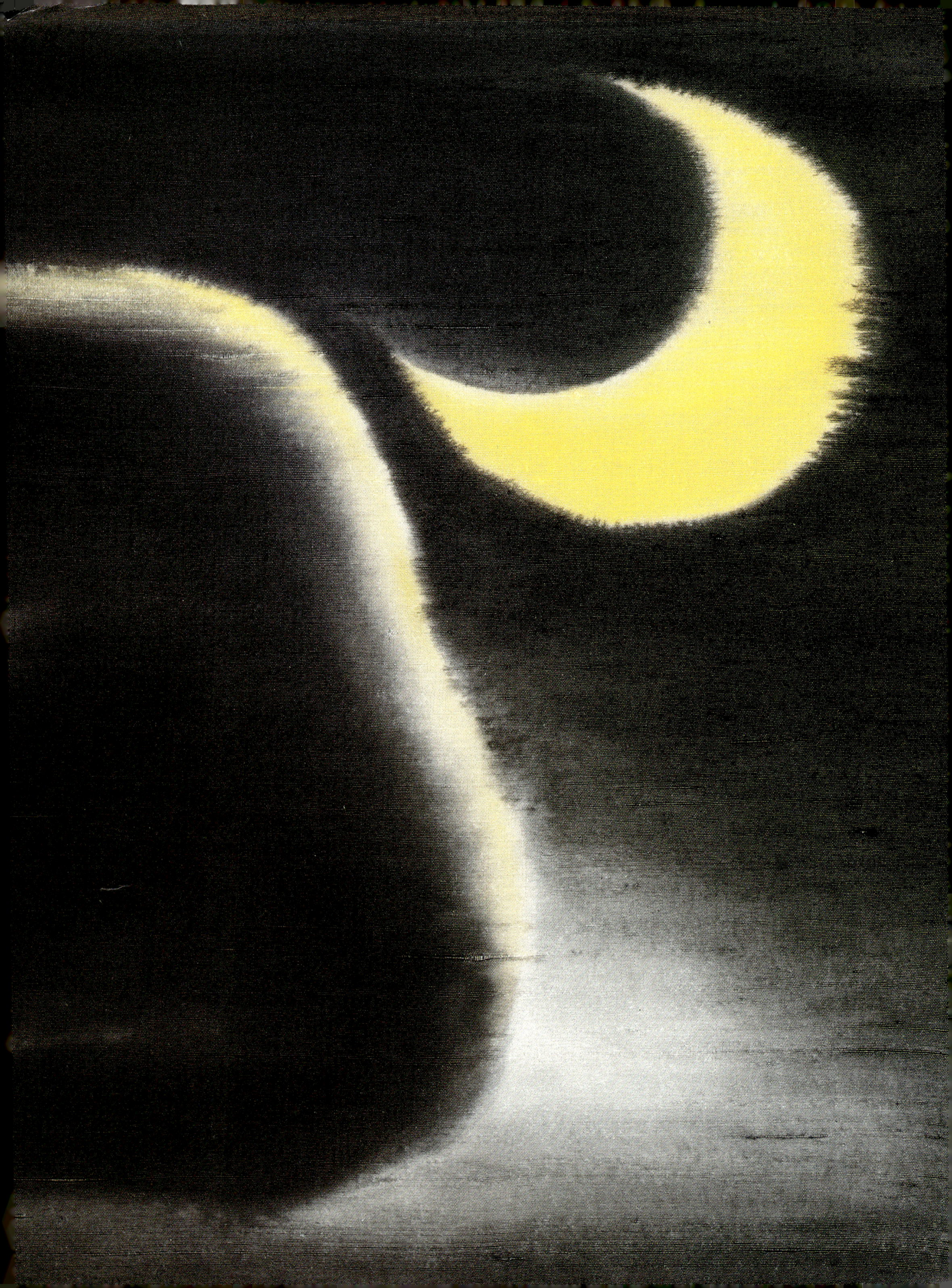

Quiet nighttime,
Quiet friend.
Soon the earth
will turn again.

Stars will fade
and sun will rise,
and I will find
some new surprise.

I have found you,
fish and owl.
I have learned
to see you now.

Snowy rabbit,
moth with eyes,
you are masters
of disguise.

Hide by sun,
and hide by moon:
but I will watch
and see you soon.

Some Notes for Older Readers

We live in a world of wonderful colors and shapes, a world we share with our animal neighbors. To the animals, color and shape often mean the difference between life and death. These natural devices help some animals to hide from predators, while the same devices help some predators to hide while they wait for their prey. Other animals are brightly colored to warn predators that they are poisonous or don't taste good. Still other animals depend on their gaudy colors to find their mates.

Camouflage

In nature, there are different ways animals avoid being easily seen. Many accomplish this by protective coloration or camouflage, a word meaning to conceal or masquerade. The pictures in this book show examples of the various ways animals are disguised to be less noticeable. The real animals in nature will look different than the ones drawn by the artist for this book, but the pictures give a good introduction to the way that animal camouflage works. The white rabbit, the snake and frog, the fish, and the owl all seem to disappear into their surroundings.

The most common kind of protective coloration is known as <u>crypsis</u>, which comes from a Greek word meaning "hidden." Although there are various ways different animals "hide," whether it is a white hare blending so well with the snow, or a spotted fawn sleeping in a meadow of flowers, the result is the same: a predator is prevented from recognizing the animals as food.

Besides blending with backgrounds or not looking like anything in particular, some other animals are colored to resemble specific things that are usually considered inedible by most predators. Some animals, especially insects, may imitate thorns, seeds, lichens (simple plants), bird droppings, and twigs or bark. When danger threatens, the "inchworm" will pretend to be invisible by stretching out and stiffening to resemble a twig. Few songbirds would want to eat a twig.

Mimicry and Warning Colors

Many different creatures that have some kind of protection, whether it is poison, a sting, or bad taste, advertise the fact by having bright warning colors. Predators have learned to leave certain boldly colored animals alone. Other animals that resemble or mimic "protected species," even though they are harmless, are also left alone by predators. Some animals, such as the caterpillar and moth, are bluffing. Their large "eyes" are only markings that startle or frighten predators such as birds that might otherwise eat them. Numerous animals mimic other animals or even plants to avoid being eaten.

Everyone who observes nature closely is rewarded by a fascinating glimpse into the natural world and the wild animals that live in it. Each new bit of information we gain about nature encourages us to learn more and to see more carefully. Our world is indeed a kaleidoscope of colors and shapes, and there may be more to see on the next bush or tree than just leaves. Look closely – there are endless surprises!

Thomas G. Smith
Director of Environmental Education, The Berkshire Museum, Pittsfield, MA.

About the pictures in this book:

Yoshi made the remarkable illustrations in this book by using a special technique of batik on silk fabric. Before starting the final illustrations, Yoshi first did careful research, as her images, though not strictly representational, are based on real forms from nature. She did some pencil sketches on paper, to plan her colors and overall designs. Next, she transferred her images to Thai silk.

In her technique, certain areas are painted with hot, melted wax. The dye will not penetrate these wax-covered areas, and the artist may either dip the fabric into a dye or apply the color by brushing it on. Yoshi uses the latter method in order to achieve the complex hues and patterns that characterize her work. The dyes come in powdered pigment form, and are mixed with water. They cannot be removed, so careful planning is essential. The wax-covered areas will be free of color once the wax is removed. However, if the wax-covered fabric is crumpled before dyeing, a pleasing marbled effect results. Yoshi also uses a sharp nail-like tool to make fine hairlines in the wax. If a soft edge is wanted, she mixes the dye with a special gum the consistency of honey. This gives the effect of a soft brush stroke, and the color will not run.

After all the painting and dyeing is done, the fabric is steamed to make the color permanent. The color does not just sit on the surface of the material – fabric and color become one. This gives the colors a depth and texture that cannot be obtained in any other way.

The illustrations when finished are very delicate. They were carefully photographed, color separations were made by a laser scanner, and they were then printed in four-color halftone, by offset lithography.

LINCOLN SCHOOL
OAK PARK, IL